THE BERENSTAIN BEARS
TO THE RESCUE

Stan & Jan

Random House

This was going to be a big day for bear scouts Brother, Sister, and Cousin Fred. To earn their Official Rescue Merit Badges, they had formed a rescue squad. Now all they had to do was find somebody to rescue.

"Finding somebody to rescue is no problem at all," said Papa. "You happen to be looking at the world's greatest rescue expert. I have rescued bears from every imaginable danger—roaring fires, raging rivers, terrible earthquakes. Just follow me and we'll find somebody to rescue pretty quick."

Papa was as good as his word. He found somebody right away. It was Grizzly Gran.

"Look!" shouted Papa. "Grizzly Gran is almost over her head in the pond! To the rescue!"

But when Papa dived into the pond, he found that Gran wasn't over her head at all. There had been a dry spell and the pond had become very shallow. Gran was simply resting on the bottom of the pond, cooling off.

"Don't you worry," said Papa after the bear scouts had pulled him out of the muck and hosed him down. "I'll help you earn your merit badges.

"Look! Right over there in Farmer Ben's meadow—Farmer Ben's daughter! She's being chased by a bull! To the rescue!"

But Papa was wrong again.
Farmer Ben's daughter was merely
leading Old Bossy out for milking.
She wasn't in the bull's pen.

Papa was! And the huge, angry bull was coming after him like an express train!

Once again the bear scouts got Papa out of trouble—this time by waving their scout hats at the bull, giving Papa a chance to escape.

The bear scouts were beginning to wonder if they were *ever* going to earn their merit badges.

"Of course you are!" said Papa. "You're going to have your chance right now! Because there's a poor chap being attacked by a swarm of angry bees!"

Once again it was Papa Bear to the rescue.

And once again it was Papa Bear in big trouble!

The "poor chap" was really Beehive Bruin, the beekeeper, and he wasn't being attacked. He was just tending his bees, which weren't a bit angry.

At least not until Papa butted in.

But the bear scouts' motto is "Be prepared," and one of the scouts whipped out a bug bomb and saved Papa from a stinging.

The scouts were becoming very discouraged.

"If we're going to earn our merit badges today, we're going to have to rescue somebody soon," said Sister Bear.

"And you will!" shouted Papa. "Because there's an unfortunate fellow trapped on a narrow ledge. One false move and he falls a thousand feet into Great Bear Gorge."

But it was Papa's footing that gave way, and over he went into Great Bear Gorge. Papa didn't fall a thousand feet. Luckily his overall suspenders caught on a scruffy tree.

The fellow on the ledge turned out to be that expert climber Professor Actual Factual Bear, out looking for rock specimens.

The bear scouts managed to pull Papa up with their trusty ropes, but they were very disappointed.

"Our efforts to earn rescue merit badges have been a complete failure," said Brother Bear. "We haven't rescued anybody!"

"Not so!" said Scout Leader Jane, who had been quietly following them. "You have rescued Papa Bear four times! And here are four Official Rescue Merit Badges—one for each of you and one for Papa. He was as good as his word. He said he'd help you earn your badges, and he did!"